D1255872

THE
SCHINOCEPHALIC
WAIF

by
ALEXANDER THEROUX · STAN WASHBURN

illustrated by

GODINE

First published in 1975 by David R. Godine, Publisher
306 Dartmouth Street, Boston, Massachusetts 02116

Text copyright © 1975 by Alexander Theroux

Illustrations copyright © 1975 by Stan Washburn

ISBN 0-87923-135-1   LCC 74-30912

Outside, it was 1554.

A waif named Gremlina, who wouldn't even smush an ant, desperately walked over the blue snows of medieval Russia on her little printless feet, seeking justice.

She had a head shaped just exactly like an onion.

Cheated by nature, Gremlina further suffered the anomalous problem of being both fat and thin-skinned. O what a swift, what an awful circuit!

"O Lost!" she cried at the grave of her parents in the potter's field and wrung her arms. Should she hurl herself into the River Bug, and simply have done?

Instead, unloved Gremlina nightly flung herself with knotted hands at the stoop of the steepleless Monastery of Our Lady of Spaso-Yefimev and humbly wailed, "Xitler, Xitler!" Meaning?

No one could say. Orphans are riddles.

But the ears of God were surely filled with sobs.

Even her little sister "Zizi," born Eupraxia, was gone, having injudiciously, one cruel frost, poisoned herself by eating some phosphorus matches she found in the way.

Meanwhile, the mighty czar, Ivan the Terrible, had sent a decree far and wee in the realm that all architects instantly come to the Kremlin and show him their new designs for the steeples of Russia. They trembled.
"I am sore afraid," said one.

"What is to be done?" screeched the czar. It was the age-old Russian question.

The Czar was around the loop with anger, kicked cushions, and gulped villainous cups of coffee, for none of the architects could answer. Heads rolled. Some were mercifully eradicated by official fire.

Everybody in court had the sullens. Even the jester, Grock the Sequesterer, cowered, having failed to amuse the Czar with his musical swinet, fulsome bellshakes, and whipt tops.

One *dryasdust functionary* presented his plan, with a church steeple shaped like a mitten. The question now was, would it wash?

"Twaddle! Artificial rain! Lesions!" howled the Czar and flung
out of the throne-room, greatly disappointed. Unhinged, some said.
Gone asiatic, said others. And some, absolutely bats.

Time passed. By day Gremlina cruised past the quays and wistfully
watched the oarage of bird's wings.

At night she wandered and with a lump in her throat searched the gutters of this exitless world for umbles, lollies, and discarded suckets, too afraid to sleep which caused bad dreams innumerable.

Of nixies, monopods, dangerous wishniks, yelpies, archdruids,
onocentaurs, kraxen, thwitchets, snools, pea-and-thimble men,

and crazed boars from the
Urals, horned, tusked,
hoofed, bristled, and
be-fanged.

Or the Frost Giants who roamed the icebound mountains.

But her worst dream wasn't one. It was real. It was her head which was shaped just exactly like an onion.

Once, a gentleman, clacking his loose wobbly dentures, set his cap at Gremlina in a dark alley, rubbed his hands, and, approaching her, likerishly whispered, "O Nymphadora, my love."

It brought a blush of shame to the cheek of modesty—until he spotted her head and, recoiling, cursed his fate in no uncertain terms.

Then one rare (i.e., sunny) day, the unhappy Czar rumbled forth past the crowd in a carriage drawn by prancing coursers, emplumed, and suddenly noticed a strange shadow cast against the snow. It was the lengthened shadow of Gremlina's head. "Halt!" he cried, in Russian. "Halt!"

People were agoggle. Through the carriage-doors a regal
finger was pointing directly at little knurled Gremlina.

Immediately, mustachioed guards in huge shakos lifted her aboard and swept her off at a gallop to the chambers of the Kremlin where she proudly sat, fresh as an apple, while the Royal Architects (those who remained) scratched away at their drawing boards night and day, repeating, "Littera occidit, spiritus vivificat."

The steeples over all Russia from that day to this, modeled on
Gremlina's head, were henceforth shaped just exactly like onions.

Gremlina, now famous and loved by all, ate buttered rockbuns, owned swans, and even went for walks in the buttongarden of the Czar, who sometimes held her hand. One afternoon, she was created a duchess.

GREMLINA

She became a bequest to the nation.